The Snow Queen

Illustrated by Eric Kincaid

SHOOTING STAR PRESS

Once there was a boy called Kay and a girl called Gerda. They were friends. They played together.

One winter's day, Kay's grandmother told them about the Snow Queen. "The Snow Queen brings the snow and ice," she said.

Kay thought he could see the
Snow Queen's face at the window.
She seemed to be calling to him.
He was afraid. He did not go.

The next day Kay went out with his sledge. He saw a bigger sledge. He tied his sledge to it for a ride.

The big sledge set off. It went
faster and faster and far away.
When the sledge stopped, Kay saw
who was driving it. It was the
Snow Queen.

The Snow Queen
kissed Kay.
"My kiss will put
ice in your
heart," she said.

"You will forget
your home.
You will forget
Gerda."
She took Kay
to her palace.

Gerda wept when she could not find
Kay. She went to the river.
"I will give you my new red shoes,"
she said to the river. "Please
tell me where Kay is."
The river said nothing.

Gerda stepped into a boat. The
boat began to move. The river was
moving the boat.

An old woman
pulled in the boat.
She cast a spell
on Gerda to make
her forget Kay.

But one day Gerda
saw a painted rose.
It made her think
of him.
"I must find Kay,"
she said and off
she ran.

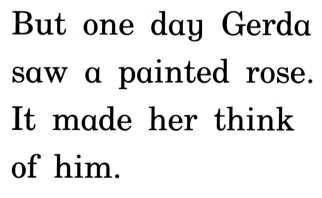

Gerda met a raven. She told the raven her story. The raven knew of a prince. "Perhaps he is Kay," said the raven.

The raven took Gerda to the palace to see the prince. But the prince was not Kay.

Gerda left the castle in a coach.

Robbers attacked the coach.
Gerda's life was saved by a little
robber girl. Gerda told the robber
girl she was looking for Kay.
The robber girl said, "I will help
you if I can."

That night a bird said to Gerda,
"I have seen Kay. He was with the
Snow Queen."
"Where were they going?" asked
Gerda.
"To the Land of Snow and Ice,"
said the bird.

"I come from that land," said
a reindeer. It belonged to the
robber girl. "I can take you
there," it said.
The robber girl agreed to set the
reindeer free.
"Take Gerda to find Kay," she said.

After many days
they came to the
Land of Snow and
Ice. They went
to see a wise
old woman.

She told the
reindeer, "You
must leave Gerda
at the Snow Queen's
garden."
The reindeer did
this.

Gerda was alone. The Snow Queen's guards tried to frighten her away. Little angels came to keep her safe.

Gerda went into
the palace. The
Snow Queen was
away. Kay was all
alone. Gerda ran
to greet him.

"Kay," she cried.
"Do you not know
me? I am Gerda."
Kay did not move
or speak. He did
not know her.

Gerda cried. Her hot tears fell
all over Kay. They melted the ice
in his heart. Now he knew who
Gerda was. Then Kay cried too.

"We must run away from here,"
said Kay. They ran to the garden.
The reindeer was waiting.

The reindeer carried them away.
They were safe from the Snow Queen
and they lived happily ever after.

All these appear in the pages of the story. Can you find them?

Kay

Gerda

Snow Queen

sledge